D0352366

C333359083

for Amy

A TEMPLAR BOOK

First published in the UK in 2011 by Templar Publishing
This softback edition published in 2013 by Templar Publishing,
an imprint of The Templar Company Limited,
Deepdene Lodge, Deepdene Avenue, Dorking, Surrey, RH5 4AT, UK
www.templarco.co.uk

Copyright © 2011 by Owen Davey

First softback edition

All rights reserved

ISBN 978-1-84877-236-6

Printed in Malaysia

templar publishing
www.templarco.co.uk

I go down the hallway...

and climb the stairs.

Then I have a bath…

and brush my teeth.

I say goodnight to Rex...

BYE

and go to my room.

I tidy away my things...

and turn out the lights.

Such a great adventure makes me very tired.

Even a knight needs a good night's sleep.